Spell Bound

Archers Beach #6

Sharon Lee

COPYRIGHT PAGE

Spell Bound
Archers Beach Number 6
© 2016 by Sharon Lee
Pinbeam Books
www.pinbeambooks.com

Will-o'-the-Wisp and *The Wolf's Bride* were previously published on Splinter Universe (www.splinteruniverse.com), January 2016
ISBN: 978-0-9966346-2-5
Published August 2016 by
Pinbeam Books
PO Box 1586
Waterville ME 04903
email info@pinbeambooks.com
cover by Sharon Lee

Will-o'-the-wisp

Felsic hadn't ever thought of herself as a coward — well. She hadn't ever thought she was brave, neither. You just did what there was to do, taking the good with the bad, like they say, and letting the sea sort it out.

That sort of thinking, now; that worked just fine for marshes and wetlands, and rivers, too, for all Felsic knew about it. Nothing so fine as a river, Felsic; just a little patch o'salt marsh, that was all. Not much to look at, and likely to smell like wet mud and rottin' reeds at low tide, but it did for her.

More than did, until just lately, when the Enterprise took a sudden interest in her, and Kate Archer no help at all.

She opened up her drawer in the dresser — and didn't that beat everything, her having a dresser drawer full of rolled socks and under clothes, and t-shirts. She'd even gone down to Dynamite and gotten herself some party clothes for tomorrow night's dance — those were in the closet. Bright red shirt, a long vest embroidered with blue, and red, and yellow flowers, and a pair of tight black trousers. Peggy'd make a face at all that color. Peggy'd be in black, like usual, but Felsic liked colors. Some folks, they said there wasn't nothin' like color in a salt marsh, but, then, some folk couldn't see past the end of their noses — not that Felsic held it against 'em. You were born blind, or you were born Sighted, and there wasn't no sense blaming either kind for being who they were.

Peggy, now, she was Sighted, and there was the problem, right there. If she hadn't been — well.

No sense dwelling on that, neither. If Peggy'd been blind-born, then she'd never seen anything other than what Felsic had wanted to her see, and the Season would've got done, and she'd gone on back down into the Flatlands — New Jersey, in particular — and Felsic'd gone back to winter with her little bit of marsh.

No dresser drawers in *that* might-be, nor party clothes, nor spooning in a tall bed, under a quilted blanket. . .leastways, not with the Season over. Felsic'd had her some good times, never you doubt it, and there wasn't no reason she couldn't've had a fine old time with Peggy Marr, and vice-versa, 'til it got time for her to go.

Except Peggy, now. Peggy'd turned out to be. . .different.

She'd never lied to Peggy. Peggy didn't hold with lying; you saw that first thing. It was just Felsic's good luck that Peggy'd never asked what it was she was, or where'd she'd lived before they'd set up house in this snug little condo, and bought all new kitchen stuff, and a sofa, and a TV set.

And that was because Peggy thought Felsic was another Kate Archer — that being her role model for people who walked off the edge of the sidewalk — just maybe without the material advantages that came with being an Archer of Archers Beach. In fact, Peggy *might've* thought that Felsic'd been rooming with Vornflee and Moss. . .an' it could just be Felsic'd given her suppositions a gentle nudge in that direction.

Wasn't lying, exactly, to let somebody have suppositions.

This now, though. She was close to a line, here, and the fact of the matter was that either side she choose, there was a lie waiting for her.

She pulled the manilla envelope out from under her t-shirts, and crossed over to the bed. Lifted the flap like the thing was like to bite her, which it hadn't done the last three times she'd had it open, and wasn't like to do now.

Inside — they were simple things. Everyday things, like mundane folk carried 'round with them in their wallets, or set aside in a file drawer and hardly thought on 'em again.

Driver's license.

Social Security card.

Birth certificate.

Every single one of 'em genuine, though Felsic was pretty sure she didn't know how to drive, and the only thing she remembered being present at her birth, backaways, was a momma mallard with a knowing button eye, who'd winked at her, then gone tail-up in the water, in search of a little something to eat.

And that there was going to be the hardest thing to explain to Peggy. Kate Archer was. . .human. Felsic was *trenvay*, born out of the needs and desires of a particular bit of geography. Felsic happened to be. . .call it the *personafication* of a little tiny corner of Scarborough Marsh, that the locals called Bufflehead Cove. Why she'd arisen — well, that was a mystery, even to Felsic. But, having gotten herself born, in the way that *trenvay* are, she'd set about the care and keeping of her bit of marsh. That'd been enough, just at first, when she'd been young and simple. But as she'd gotten older, and stronger, her horizons had widened, in a matter of speaking. That just naturally came with age, so far as Felsic'd seen. Why, Kate Archer's Gran'd been born a dryad, and tied tight to her tree. And now she had some years on her, didn't she just wander all over town?

So, Felsic'd begun to take an interest, which she had to, the Beach having been without a proper Guardian for so long — and the result of all her care and effort being —

A driver's license, a birth certificate, a Social Security card. . .

. . .and a proper name.

Francis Eleanor Sicot, so it said on the paper, born to one Willow Jane Sicot, no father listed, at the South Portland Medical Center, about thirty years ago, which put her near enough to Peggy's age. On paper, leastways.

Lies, every bit of it, even if there'd been a Willow Jane Sicot, who'd gone and got herself in trouble. It was in her to wonder where was Willow Jane now, and if maybe she might need a hand — and she shook herself, hard.

There was a brisk tap on the door. She snatched up the papers, like she was going to hide them again — then let them fall back onto the bed. Past time for hiding, she told herself sternly; you're almost into lying.

"Felsic?" Peggy's voice came through the door. "You OK?"

She took a deep breath, looked down, and turned toward the door.

"Almost," she said, wryly, and feeling her stomach grab up into a knot.

"Whyn't you come on in, Peg? There's some things you gotta know."

#

"So you're telling me that these papers here are — counterfeit? That somebody here in town made them?"

Peggy shook her head and put the Social Security card down on the bedspread next to the other papers.

"Damn, I wish I'd know about this back at the beginning of the Season. I wouldn't have had to play quite so many games with Arbitrary and Cruel's hiring policies."

"You'd've ordered in false IDs for the whole crew?" Felsic asked, momentarily diverted.

"You're thinking it would've been expensive? I had an expense account and total discretion. By the time they did the audit, the Season would've been over." She looked thoughtful, lips pursed.

"More or less the same result, actually," she said, and shrugged. "So, Felsic, if these papers are — counterfeit. . .I guess I'd like to know why you need counterfeit papers?"

"That's a good question. Kate's of the opinion that I'm on the edge of getting more responsibility on the Beach. The kind of responsibility that needs a Social Security card to be listened to."

"*Kate* gave you these?"

Her tone said she didn't believe it, and Felsic didn't blame her. Truth said, Kate'd looked as horrified as Felsic, when she'd opened up the envelope. 'course, Kate had some idea of how unsettling the Enterprise was, just as a general concept, which Peggy didn't.

"Kate offered to talk to you about how them papers come in," she said. "I don't understand it, myself — not that I think Kate does. Her edge over us is she's seen it done more'n once."

Peggy nodded.

"I'll keep it in mind," she said slowly, and reached out to tap the birth certificate.

"But if this is counterfeit — who are you really?"

Well, now, that was the question, wasn't it?

Felsic took a hard breath, feeling chill all the way up from the bottom of her feet to the top of her head.

Peggy. . .There was some things even the Sighted shouldn't ought to see, and the first. . .

"Felsic," she said, quietly. "You know I won't get mad, so long as you tell me the truth."

Mad, no. But there was plenty of room for horror, and other kinds of upset that she'd never willingly bring Peggy to feel.

Shoulda been smarter, Felsic told herself, but there wasn't any way to go back to the first of the Season, and seein' her for the first time, and feeling that tug that meant here was a prize worth having. .

.

"You promise me something," she said suddenly, and knew by the change on Peggy's face that her voice had been every bit as harsh as she'd feared.

"What's that?"

"You promise me, if you need to leave — to leave this house, on account of what truth I'll be showing you. If you need to leave here, you'll go to Kate Archer, and tell 'er."

Peggy frowned.

"Tell her what?"

"You'll know what, if you gotta say it out," Felsic said with certainty, and looked down at the documents spread over their bed. She used her chin to point at the driver's license.

"That right there's your first lie," she said. "That photograph. I don't — the real me ain't quite so. . .smooth."

She turned to the chest of drawers, facing the mirror there. Peggy'd see the reflection over her shoulder. She didn't stop to wonder why she thought that might be less upsetting than seeing it straight.

There was a face in the mirror — an easy, comfortable face that she wore for those who didn't believe in magic, or creatures of the night, or spirits of the place. That face was glamour, and that's *all* it was. Sugar-coating, if you like it that way.

Her real face. . .well, she'd been born out of the will of a piece of marshland, now hadn't she? Marsh had the general shape of things, but it'd been a little foggy on details.

That being so, her real face was what you might call rugged: broad and flat; nose not much more'n a bump; no chin to speak of; and a wide, thin-lipped mouth. Her eyes were deep, and dark; the rest of her shape following the broad, flat design.

She took a breath, staring into her own eyes, and breathed out, releasing the glamour, part of her waiting for Peggy to scream.

Except that the face in the mirror didn't change. It remained obstinately round, with an adorable uptilted nose, generous mouth, and a sturdy chin. Only the eyes were as they should be — dark as bog water, with glimmers of cinnamon in the depths. Her shape was strong; broad in the shoulders, and sturdy at the waist; and the tshirt clung somewhat to definite breasts.

Felsic felt a little stutter of horror all her own.

Behind her, she heard the bedclothes shift, then Peggy was behind her in the mirror, arms around her waist.

"Hey, nobody's license photo is any good," she said. "You should see mine. No, on second thought, you shouldn't. I don't want to scare you."

Felsic leaned back into Peggy's hug, and tried to think.

The Enterprise was powerful, and unpredictable; everybody knew that — *trenvay* and townie alike. You didn't ask, that was it, and if you were lucky, the Enterprise didn't answer, anyway.

But it had taken an interest in her, and somehow, by. . .taking delivery of those papers, she'd gotten. . .nailed into place. Woven into the warp and woof of the mundane world; her aspect fixed —

And her duty? Her little bit of marsh, that was her life, and her reason for being born?

"Felsic?"

"Peg, I'm not. . .like you," she said.

"Right, you're like Kate — which is to say that you're an extra-special person with powers of which I wot not. I don't mean to imply that you and Kate are interchangeable. For one thing, she's straight."

And it had used to be that Felsic was neither one kind nor another, pleasure being pleasure, and the marsh not expecting to deliver or sire children. Didn't seem any way to exactly explain that, either. Felsic bent her head, stomach cramped and unhappy. She put her hands over Peggy's where they were caught together at her waist, and squeezed.

"You're upset," Peggy said quietly. "What else do you need to tell me?"

Felsic swallowed.

Papers, she thought. She had papers, now, and the papers trapped her in a lie — except, what had Kate said? That the papers brought *additional* duty. Her primary duty, that was still with her. She wasn't mundane, not wholly. What those papers made her was — a little more visible to those who were generally blind.

That was all right. Well. With work, and some help from the Guardian of Archers Beach, it could be made to be all right. But that — *them*. Those half-blind folk, they weren't where her heart was. Peggy. . .

Peggy not only wanted the truth; she *needed* to have the truth.

Felsic shivered. Other *trenvay* knew where to find her — where to find *her soul*, she guessed the marsh must be, which was a funny old thought, and not one she remembered having before. The Guardian surely knew where to find her. But, she'd never shown herself — her soul — to anyone. . .mundane. Never, in all the winters she'd been alive.

"Show you," she said hoarsely.

"What?"

Felsic cleared her throat.

"There's a thing I gotta show you," she said, and lifted her head, catching Peggy's eyes in the mirror.

"Right now, before I lose my nerve."

#

"Here."

"Here?"

They were holding hands, standing side-by-side on a piece of marsh that, to Peggy's eyes, Felsic figured, looked pretty much like every other piece of marsh they'd walked through to get to this one spot, where Felsic's blood jumped with joy, and of a sudden she was wide, and deep; and slow and secret. Grasses tickled her ribs, and crabs scuttled along her skin; she felt a harrier land on a bush just over there, heard the scream of a frog pierced by a heron. . .

"Tell me about it," Peggy said quietly.

Felsic blinked at her.

"Don't know there's much to tell," she said, and her voice was slow, and deeper, too, like the voice of the dark waters all around. "I can name off the plants, if you like it, or –"

"Tell me what you're feeling," Peggy said.

And so Felsic told her about the tickling salt hay, and the hurrying crabs, the slow fish, the intensity of the hunting heron, and the hawk fair sitting on her shoulder. They moved along, still hand-in-hand, Felsic making sure the mud supported Peggy, while she showed her where, come spring, there'd be aster, and bayberry; wild orchid and blueberries. . .

"We're getting ready for the long sleep," she said. "Hay's starting to die back, like you see. Pretty soon now the visitor birds'll be leaving; the muskrats an' all that sort'll be settling into dens. Not so much for a *trenvay* to do, 'cept keep good watch, an' be sure nobody with his brains in his pants comes through here with a snowmachine, or, worse, a four-wheeler.

"Old days, first snow, I'd just settle in to sleep myself. Some still do. Others of us, we come to keep more active watch in the winter. There's more things can go wrong lately, and they just don't happen in the warm days."

She heard those last words, and came to the realization that she'd been talking along, heedless, for. . .quite some while, telling Peggy all about it, like she'd asked.

Stomach clenched, she turned and looked down into violet eyes, which were looking steadfastly up into her face.

Felsic thought she might ought to say something — and then thought that she'd already said more'n enough.

She swallowed.

Peggy smiled and reached up to touch her cheek.

"I love you," she said.

#

"So, who's Willow Jane Sicot?" Peggy asked. It was a couple days after their walk in the marsh, and the end-of-Season party. They were sitting at the bar in their kitchen, sharing a third cup of coffee.

It took Felsic a tick to recall the name; then she shrugged.

"Something the Enterprise snatched outta the wind, I'm guessing. Person with a driver's license and a Social, she's gotta at least have had a mother."

Peggy frowned.

"Kate seemed to think that the Enterprise — or whoever writes out those papers and *sends them in* — works within reality. It might've gotten away with making up a mother, before computerized record-keeping and all our –" She made quote marks in the air — "*modern day improvements*, but not anymore. I'm betting there is — or at least *was* — a Willow Jane."

"Could be," Felsic said. "Don't see that it has much of anything to do with me."

"Do you mind if I look around?" Peggy asked. "I'm curious."

Felsic grinned.

"You ain't got enough to do with getting Fun Country in shape to open in April?"

Peggy opened her eyes wide.

"What, that? That's a piece of cake, and I could eat it in my sleep. This thing with your mom — that's *interesting*."

"*My mom*, is it?" Felsic shook her head, between amusement and concern. "Peggy, you know –"

She held up a hand.

"I know, I know. Born of the marsh in service of the marsh. Not even technically human. You said it. Kate said it. You're the experts. But — I'm still curious. You don't mind?"

"No. . ." said Felsic, and told herself that she didn't.

#

"Turn right here," Peggy said.

Felsic obediently slowed the Prius, put on the right turn signal, and made a slow, careful turn into a skinny driveway near overgrown with box cedar. She steered the car carefully — she'd been practicing daily, sometimes with Peggy, other times with Kate, and on one occasion with Cap'n Borgan himself, who'd actually managed to squeeze his big self into the Prius' front seat.

Despite all that practice, she still wasn't best friends with the idea of driving a car, and if left to herself, she'd rather walk anywhere she needed to go.

This, now; this was supposed to've been a practice drive, out Route 9 to 1, but it seemed like Peggy'd changed her mind.

The drive opened up into little half-moon parking lot, with lines marking spaces for eight cars; three had cars in them.

Facing the parking lot was low building with faded blue shingles, and a sign over the double glass doors.

"*Maison de la mer*?" Felsic said. "What're we needing at the House of the Sea, Peg?"

"Jane W. Sicot lives here," Peggy said, and when Felsic didn't say anything back right away, on account of having to sort through why the name was important, she added, "Your mother."

"Thought my mother was Willow Jane Sicot." Felsic was on firm ground, now. "And only on a piece of paper, at that."

"People change their names around. Turns out that Jane W. is Jane Willow; she confirmed that when I spoke to her on the phone. Willow's a family name."

"You talked to her on the phone?" Felsic repeated, feeling her stomach clench up tight.

Peggy looked at her, straight and stern.

"You said you didn't mind if I tried to find her."

"And nor yet, I don't. I don't recall ever being asked, *did I want to meet her* if you did find her."

There was a small silence.

"That's fair," Peggy said; "we didn't discuss that. Would you like to meet Jane W. Sicot, Felsic?" She looked around at the mostly empty parking lot, the battered building in need of paint, and the sign over the double doors.

"It doesn't look like anybody here gets a lot of company."

#

The room was empty, except for the lone figure in the wheelchair overlooking the autumn marsh, and a bunch of metal chairs, folded up and leaning against the wall.

"She's always here," the nurse said in an undertone. "The night nurse says some shifts she comes through and there she is, in the window, and there can't be anything to see at night! I mean, look at it! There's hardly anything to see in broad daytime!"

Peggy squeezed Felsic's hand gently. Neither one answered the nurse, though Felsic thought the woman in the chair showed good sense. Who *wouldn't* prefer a view of the marsh to the various activity rooms they'd passed on the way from the front of the building to the back.

"Jane?" the nurse said brightly. "You have visitors!"

The figure did not turn from her contemplation of the marsh. Felsic approved. Who were they, anyways, to interrupt her?

Peggy, though, had a different idea. She strode forward, pulling Felsic with her.

"Ms. Sicot, I'm Peggy Marr. I called you yesterday, and you said it would be all right for my friend and me to stop by today for a chat."

The figure turned the chair, slowly, pale October light falling across a ravaged pale face, and glittering in short white hair.

"That's right," she said, and her voice was fine and firm. "Pull up some chairs, and set a spell. Rachel," she said, apparently to the nurse; "thank you."

"Now, you know it's no trouble. Can I bring you anything? A blanket? It's chilly in here, isn't it?"

"I'm comfortable," said Ms Sicot.

The nurse hesitated, then nodded and went away.

Peggy grabbed a folding chair, and Felsic did. They carried them back to the window and unfolded them, facing the woman in the wheelchair.

"Thank you for agreeing to see us, Ms. Sicot," Peggy said.

"It's not like I've got much else to do," the old woman said. "Call me Jane, please. Now, what's this about a daughter?"

Peggy extended a hand and touched Felsic on the sleeve. Ms. — Jane's eyes followed the motion.

"This is my partner, Francis Eleanor Sicot," Peggy said.

The white head inclined formally.

"Francis."

"Friends call me Felsic, ma'am," she said easily, and leaned forward a little, looking like a *trenvay* looks, with something more than mundane seeing, and saw that the woman — this Jane — was old, and sick. Sick to death; Felsic saw it plain, and the time she had left less than a single hand of days.

Dying, and her preferred companion was nothing more or less than Scarborough Marsh.

"Felsic, then. You think you might be my daughter?"

"No, ma'am. Peggy thinks that. She's got a mother, see, and she just naturally don't want me to be without anything she finds good."

Peggy made a sound like a sneeze. Jane Sicot smiled.

"That's what love is; wanting good things for your better half. I assume you *are* the better half?"

"No'm, I'm nothing such. Peggy's the best of both of us."

Another sneeze, and Peggy's fingers pressed hard around her wrist.

The smile widened, then faded.

"What I'm thinking," Felsic continued; "and I hope you'll excuse me, if I'm rude — what I'm thinking is you might be a little long in the years to be my mother. Birth certificate has the name as Willow Jane Sicot."

Jane Sicot tensed in her chair. It was the Marsh let Felsic feel how her heart stuttered, though why the Marsh would trouble itself. . .

"Willow Jane Sicot," Jane repeated, and sighed, her heartbeat more even now, though slow and tired. She smiled, though it wobbled 'round the edges.

"I don't think you're rude at all, Felsic — in fact, you're right. I am not young enough to be your mother." She took a breath.

"But I'm plenty old enough to be your grandmother."

#

"Willow Jane. . .she was a good girl, not a mean bone in her body. She'd been born with — well, back then, they called *mongolism*, and it wasn't expected that those who had it would live much past little children. Back then, they said, too, that the best place for such children was in an institution. Well! It don't take any great mind to connect the dots there, and I figured, if Willow wasn't to live long, she ought to be loved and looked after like any little child, in her own home, with her parents caring for her.

"So we brought her home. Our house was right on the edge of the Marsh. The mister, he fished, and I did the books for the 'change from my kitchen table, and I kept Willow right by me." She smiled, then, dreamy with memory.

"She was a happy baby, and I was certain I'd made the right decision, to bring her home, to be inside of her family, for as long as she had."

"Problem was, the mister didn't warm to Willow, despite she was his daughter. And finally of a day just after her fourth birthday, he said to me that she'd be better off in a home, is what he called it. And, well, that was a choice, right there, and me — I chose Willow."

She leaned back in her chair and closed her eyes.

Felsic felt Peggy stir next to her.

"Mrs. Sicot, you don't have to —"

Jane Sicot opened her eyes.

"No, you're wrong there. I do have to. This has a point that concerns you, and — well, Peggy Marr, you were right to call me. There's not much story left, and I think all three of us'll be better for hearing it."

Peggy sighed.

"Felsic?"

"We asked," Felsic said, reaching out to take her hand. "Only polite to hear the answer."

"Thank you."

Another rest against the chair; another series of slit-eyed, shallow breaths.

"Come to it, Willow lived past childhood, she lived through being a teenager. There wasn't any question of sending her to school;

I taught her what I could, at home. We still lived right there on the edge of the Marsh, and she wandered there, most days; never come to harm. I was still doing the books for the Fisherman's Exhange, and for some of the fishermen, too. Made enough for the two of us, and the neighbors helped keep the house in repair."

She paused.

This now, Felsic thought; *this* is the painful part, even worse than the mister left them, for cause of not being able to love his own daughter.

"One afternoon, she didn't come home, and I was so absorbed in unknotting Caleb Varney's quarterlies, that I didn't even miss her until it was full dark.

"I went out looking, and — and I found her, not far. Short of it, she'd been beaten, and raped, and just left there in the mud. . ."

Hard breath.

"Eight months later, there was a baby. By then, we had Social Services in it, like we'd never had, all the years before, with their clipboards, and their rules. . .

"It was the Social Service caseworker who told me that Willow's baby had died, not five minutes after the nurse came to tell me that Willow was gone, herself."

Jane Sicot shook her head.

"I believed her — Social Services — and it didn't strike me odd 'til later, that nobody'd brought that baby to me, so she could be buried with her mother. And when I asked, Social Services said the hospital had taken care of it; and the hospital referred me to Social Services. . ."

She met Felsic's eyes, hers damp.

"That's bothered me for a lot of years, now."

Felsic nodded.

"I can see it would."

"You got the look of her, a little, and if you got a birth certificate with her name on it — I guess they must've fostered you out?"

"I had good care," Felsic told her, gentle as she could, and mindful of Peggy, who knew the truth, and valued the telling of it. "I was wanted, and I couldn't've asked for no better life than I've had."

Jane Sicot smiled.

"Good. That's good."

"I'm sorry," Peggy said softly.

Jane Sicot turned her head. She was smiling, slightly.

"Nothing to be sorry for, Peggy Marr. I'm glad you called, and I'm glad you brought her to me. Now, if you'll do me a favor, like I done you — I'd like a few minutes to talk to Felsic alone. If you wanna walk slow back to the front desk, and tell 'em I'm wantin' that blanket after all, and you'll bring it along to me, that'll be time enough."

"Felsic?" Peggy said. "You'll be all right?"

Why she wouldn't be all right alone with a woman too sick to raise her arm was more than Felsic could figure, but it was like Peggy to want to know she'd feel safe, and so she gave a smile, and a nod.

"I'll be fine, Peg."

"All righty, then. One blanket the slow way, coming up."

She rose and left them, walking briskly until she reached the hall, when her pace changed to a light-footed stroll, nothing like her usual businesslike stride.

Felsic grinned again, and turned back to Jane Sicot, who was looking at her closely.

"Willow used to tell me about her friends, in the Marsh," she said. "Pretty lights, and mist shaped like people that you could see right through, and otters who would come up and sun themselves on a rock and tell her a story. I thought — well, I thought it was made up, who wouldn't think that?"

Felsic didn't say anything.

"I thought that," Jane Sicot said, "until the night she didn't come home. I ran out into the Marsh — it was pitch, and there was more chance that I'd fall and break an ankle then there was of finding her. I called, though, and I wandered, and was prolly lost myself, when, up from the weeds come a glowing ball, all blue and gold and friendly seeming, and I know *you'll* believe me when I say that glowing ball led me straight to where he'd left her, bleeding and broken, and covered in mud. Took me straight there, and then lighted me back to the house. I looked back, when I got to the door, and it was there, like it was watching. I pushed the door open and it — blinked out."

Felsic nodded.

"This doesn't surprise you," said Jane Sicot.

"No, ma'am."

"Can you see these things, too? Like. . .your mother did?"

"I can see 'em, yes, ma'am." She paused, her eyes straying over the sick woman's shoulder to the marsh. Sat here all the time, did she? Even in the dark night-time?

"You can see 'em, too, I think."

She met the other woman's eyes.

A slow nod.

"They give me drugs, you know. For the pain. I'm not really sure what I'm seeing, not always, but it's certain that whatever it or they are, they're not going to come in and talk with me."

Felsic nodded again.

"We're shy, some of us; others of us, we're young."

"Us?" repeated Jane. "You're magic, then, are you?"

"No'm; I'm the most natural thing there is, all us Marsh-folk are. We each take care of our own little bit o'business. Me, now, I'm Bufflehead Cove, right back from the Seagull in Archers Beach. Other thing you need to know is — I'm old. Way too old for you to've been my gran, nor your girl m'mother — though I wouldn't have minded if it'd gone that way."

Jane laughed, short and breathy.

"I don't think I would've minded it, either."

She moved the fingers of her right hand, like she was asking Felsic to move closer.

"Tell me what it's like, being Bufflehead Cove."

She thought about that for a minute, remembering back to the day she'd taken Peggy into the Marsh. Then she leaned forward, took one wracked, cold hand between both of hers, looked into the dark, too-bright eyes, raised her glamour, and *showed* her.

It wasn't done, not usually; you didn't want to set a mundane running mad. But Jane Sicot was dying. It could've been that the drugs made it easier for her to See, or the dying itself. Anywise, for a whole turn of seasons that lasted only four minutes by the mundane clock, Jane Sicot *was* Bufflehead Cove, every stone, every tiny green crab, every tall, stalking blue heron. She rose and fell in the sluggish, salty water, and the wind combed her salt hay hair. Sunlight beat down upon her, drying the mud, and she put forth blossoms, and blueberries, and felt the leaves peel away in the cold wind, while the hay withered, and the snow came down upon her, and she slept.

She slept.

Footsteps struck Felsic's ear. She sat up, still holding Jane's hand, and turned her head to watch Peggy come down the room, blanket over one arm.

"Is she. . ."

"Asleep, is all." Felsic laid the ravaged hand on a thin knee, and stood to help Peggy drape the blanket 'round her shoulders.

"Should we say good-bye?" Peggy asked.

"I'd say let her sleep," Felsic said, and she nodded.

They folded up the chairs, put them quietly back against the wall, and walked out of the building.

"What did she want to ask you?" Peggy said, when they'd gotten into the car.

"She'd caught sight of some of the marsh *trenvay*," Felsic said. "Wanted to know what it was like."

"And you told her?"

"I showed her. Figured it couldn't do any harm."

She turned suddenly in her seat.

"Peggy?"

"Yes?"

"Thank you," Felsic said. "I'm glad you brought me down here for this."

"Not mad?"

"Not even," said Felsic, and leaned forward.

"Love you," she said, and their kiss was all the magic she could ever need.

−end−

Author's Notes
Will-o'-the-wisp

Peggy Marr arrives in Archers Beach during *Carousel Sun*. She's employed by Fun Country Corporate, which she tends to refer to as Arbitrary and Cruel, and it's her job to get the midway portion of Fun Country up and running for the Season, on an impossibly short schedule. She's a strong, tough realist, despite the fact that she's able to See, just a little way, into the Wyrd.

Now, when I was writing *Carousel Sun*, I knew that the new manager for the Midway was going to be a plot point. I didn't know how, or who, mind you; I tend to let these things work themselves out on their own. But, in broad form, I knew Peggy Marr — or somebody like Peggy Marr — was going to be part of the story.

The surprise — was Felsic.

Now, I knew — sort-of-knew, say — that the new manager of the Midway was going to have to cope with *trenvay* — hadn't written "The night don't seem so lonely" yet, but I kinda, sorta knew, and without really looking too closely, that the Midway was pretty much completely run by *trenvay*.

What I hadn't expected that there would be a sort of straw-boss *trenvay*, who kept the troops more-or-less in order in the absence of the Guardian — and who would find somebody like Peggy Marr. . .irresistible.

Felsic and Peggy are continuing characters, and their relationship grows during *Carousel Seas*, at the end of which Felsic receives this packet holding papers which declare her to be a Real Girl, to her very mixed feelings.

I hope you enjoyed the story of what came after.

—Sharon Lee

January 2016

The Wolf's Bride

The dogs of the village knew him; and he passed without challenge from forest edge to market street, walking with a predator's sure, silent tread down the moss-lined way.

Above, the night-time sky was a velvet stole, across which a handful of jewels had been scattered, winking in bright hues of gold, and green, and blue. It was silent in the darkness, as it never was in the day, when the merrybells sang the sun's praises. His bones told him that it was mid-night, and he lengthened his stride, then breathed a laugh at his own foolishness.

He had meant to be earlier. Indeed, he had meant to arrive at the sun's height, with leisure to stop by his own small house to bathe and attire himself in what finery he possessed, so that he might come seemly before the headwoman.

Well, and now he had more than ample leisure to bathe and make himself fine, for the headwoman would surely not rise for some hours yet, and if he was wise — which he could be — he would allow her time to break the night's fast, and drink a bracing cup, or two, of thistle tea before he approached her with his topic.

Thus occupied with his thoughts, he came to the main square; the village cistern a squat shadow against the night's velvet; and the merrypole a dark lance driven upward toward the stars.

Another shape, lithe, hesitant, and faintly limned in green detached from the greater bulk of the cistern.

Her scent traveled to him on the breeze, but she was fleeter yet, hesitation flung to the stars, as she raced silent across the mossy square. His bow was slung; all he need do was open his arms, and catch her as she flew into them.

"Cael!"

They were much of a height; she stood on her toes to grasp another few inches, and brought her mouth down on his.

Her kiss was a complex thing; demanding, angry, relieved; then nuance was lost as his blood heated and he returned her passion with his own.

"Ah!"

She pulled away first, settling onto flat feet, her hands on his shoulders, her gaze holding his, for she saw as sharply in the dark as in the day, did his Senaya; and he had a hound's keen vision.

"I looked for you earlier," she said; and, "I was worried."

"I had looked to arrive earlier," he answered; and, "Never worry, love."

"If you would stand away from desperate ventures, perhaps I would learn not to worry!"

That was merely the last flames of a fiery temper, ignited by her fear. Senaya was bold; fearless on her own behalf. For him, though, she feared, as if he still had his milk teeth.

"What happened?" she asked then; "to delay you?"

"A old ram charged a young shepherd, after the dogs had done. We were called back, to mend the line, and bring the runaways home."

She looked disbelieving, as well she might.

"The ram took four ewes with him; and the four ewes each took a lamb. They led us a dance. After, the master would have it that I had mismanaged the thing and thought to withhold a portion of my wage."

She stirred in his arms.

"Never mind; he thought better of it."

Senaya laughed.

"Yes, I expect he did — and quickly, too!"

Laughter lit her face, and this time it was he who kissed her.

"Well, then," he said, eventually, and just as if herding goats from my lord Aeronymous' honor to that of Lord Eredith was dangerous beyond reckoning. . .

"My last chancy venture is complete. Tomorrow, I will offer myself to the headwoman and to Seafort."

She relaxed against him and lay her head on his shoulder with a sigh.

"And we may be married."

Senaya was the headwoman's third daughter. Her gift was herbalism, and healing, which placed her high in the village's regard. He. . .was not of the village, though he had lived within it all his life. *His* mother, no one knew; nor his father. His foster mother had been a ranger, and one day had brought him back from the forest, with a tale of having found him in a wolf's den, naked, and with gnawed bones all about him.

It had been his foster mother who held shy of giving him to the village. Best, she had told him, that he make that decision, when he was old enough to know himself.

Well. His foster mother had her own foibles, and there had some old matter that lay between her and the headwoman. Some seasons back, she had married, herself, and chose to go to her spouse's village. He had been on his own by then, established in his own small house. He had helped her pack what few items she would take with her, and to unmake the house that had been hers. Together, they had sung the memories out of the ground, and sowed heart's-ease and blanc-mallow, to freshen it for the next to build there.

He might have offered himself to the village anytime after establishing his own residence, but there had been pride involved. He would not come as a pauper; and, when it came plain that Senaya returned his regard, he had determined to come to her as an equal, and not only as "the healer's chosen."

Pride was satisfied, now, and tomorrow all would be put to right. They had decided between them that their first act as bond-mates would be to take his house down and rebuild it as a part of hers, making the single dwelling, in truth, *their* house.

He sighed.

"Regrets?"

"That it is not tomorrow evening, perhaps. No others."

She laughed, and stirred in his arms.

"Come," she said, standing back and catching his hand. "Let us see you to bed. For I will tell you plainly, my Cael, that, even should you miss the headwoman tomorrow day, you will in no way be safe from me, tomorrow night!"

"That seems no threat at all," he protested, allowing her to pull him across the square.

"You have not yet heard what I will do to you!" Senaya told him, and laughing, they skipped like children, under the stars.

#

The headwoman was the heart and the life of Seafort Village; she was the repository of the village's combined power; their defender and their solace. This was the natural order of things, that the weaker ceded their power to the strongest, who conserved it for everyone and wielded it when necessary.

Being a power, the headwoman glowed, even in the bright daylight, with the merrybells in full tongue. She glowed, and she frowned, and she continued to do both, even after he had said what was in his heart, and bowed to her honor. No word passed her lips, and he felt neither the thrill of her power passing through him, nor the ache of his, being drawn.

Perhaps, he thought, he had mis-done the thing. Perhaps, she waited to learn if he was fully and wholly set upon this path.

Reasoning thus, he called his own meager power, shivering, though it rose hot, as always; breathed in to center himself before opening —

"Hold."

The word was spoken quietly; the headwoman rarely raised her voice. Rarely, too, did she speak a Word, unless it was truly needed. He did not think she spoke such now, though he felt a little sting, as if she had lashed his pride.

Straightening, he allowed his power to fall back to its nesting place at the base of his spine, and met the headwoman's emerald eyes full on.

She smiled, then, and nodded; for she had ever been one to admire boldness.

"You would have the thing done, and quickly," she said. "I understand your impatience. And yet I must ask you, Cael Sojourner, if you have thought this matter through." Her smile came again.

"With your head, understand me. I do not often advise others to discount Senaya, but I counsel you, if you find it possible, to set her to one side of your considerations."

He paused for three long breaths, that he not seem over-hasty in his reply, then made answer.

"Mother, I would have offered myself any time these last six seasons. I have lived here for all of my life that I recall. Who else would I come to, save the folk, and the place, that has sheltered me so long?"

"And yet you did not offer yourself until now," she said; "what held you away?"

He sighed.

"Pride. I would not come a beggar, with nothing, in fact, to give to the commonweal, save my weakness and my need."

"And now you stand before me possessed of a respectable store of power, and none may say that Cael took more than he gave. I understand. And yet, there is this matter of your. . .other attributes, which are warp and woof of Cael — power, surely! But not as we measure or know it."

"Mother, I –"

"Peace," she said mildly, and pointed at the stool near her feet. "Sit. My neck is cricked with staring up at you."

He sat, arranging his legs about the little stool, and gazed up into her face as fair and round as the moon.

"Your foster mother and I too often saw past each other, but in this instance, I agreed with her. You will recall that she did not give you to the village, but maintained that the choice be yours, when you came to know yourself fully."

She looked at him sharply and he bowed his head.

"I recall it," he said, and pressed his lips together before he uttered *but. . .*

"You know that this village looks to my Lord Aeronymous; that we live within his honor and under his protection?"

He stared at her. Of course, he knew this; how could he not? Still, it seemed she waited for his answer, so he gave it, soft-voiced and patient as he might be.

"Yes, Mother, I know these things."

"Then have you taken thought — have you taken counsel of — this other power of yours, which is beyond us, and so much a part of you that you scarce understand it for power? Do you wish to place that power — whatever it is — in the service of my Lord Aeronymous, Cael Sorjourner?"

"Mother –"

"Stay a moment and *think*! You might remain among us as always you have been — a guest, surrounded by our goodwill, giving to your host of yourself, as a good guest will, but. . .unremarked by my Lord; strange as they are, your powers would thus be protected by your solitary nature."

Such a solitary nature would mean that he could not share himself with. . .anyone.

Senaya.

Pain lanced through him, that they might not, that they never could complete their bonding. For what did he preserve himself, if his life thus became ashes and dust?

He raised his face to say this to the headwoman — and saw resignation in her face.

"I feared it would be thus. As the conscience and the protector of the village, I cannot but accept your gift freely given. My daughter has made her wishes plain; there is no one and nothing that might gainsay her. Certainly not her mother, who will be proud to welcome so able a son into her house — and a man of power into her village."

She extended her hands, palms up.

Cael placed his palms against hers, and felt his power rise. He gasped when a tithe of it left him, to bond with the headwoman's power. . .

And gasped again as her power flowed back, accepting; and tying him to the village.

"It is done" she said, then, lifting her hands away. "Go and be happy, Cael of Seafort."

#

Happy he was, and fortunate, too. He and Senaya brought their houses together as they had planned, and all the village joined to sing them into harmony.

As for the bond he shared with Senaya — he could not imagine life without that deep and certain source of love and strength. He wondered that he could have stood solitaire for so long. Surely, had he known the fullness of what he would share with Senaya, his pride would have melted before the knowledge.

Senaya, of course, served the village as healer and herbalist, just as before. He, having foresworn dangerous employment that took him beyond the ken of Seafort Village, cast about him for a needed service that met his skills.

He was able, and trained by his foster mother, thus he took up the jacket and the duties of a ranger. The forest of younger trees close to the village was generally safe enough, though willie wisps and other vermin would sometime venture near. Stranger things tended to arise beneath the elder trees, though, and it was the duty of the rangers to scout those territories and turn the strangest aside, far before they should endanger peaceful Seafort.

Indeed, he was precisely at the margin between the tame forest, hard by, but not within, the feral shadow of the elder trees, one fine mid-day. There had been market-day rumors regarding a child of the elder trees that perhaps had become over-bold, and approached the roads and outlying farmsteads too nearly.

He might have discounted such tales as boredom-bred, but the dogs of the village confided to him certain exotic scents, and unlikely sounds heard inside the night, at dawn-time, and sunset.

Those reports, he took seriously; much more so than the whispered tales of a shadow glimpsed by a farm-hedge, or the print of an unnatural foot in the clay by the edge of the river.

That morning, he had found the scent the dogs had given him at the village ward-stones, when he had crossed into the forest. It was fresh, and he followed, thinking to catch his quarry well before they came to the elder trees.

But the quarry's wood-lore was superior to his own; it gained the safety of its parent trees before Cael caught more than one troubling glimpse of it. Whereupon, he stood at the edge of the old forest, home of dangerous trees who held no love for his kind, and wondered whether he ought to follow. . .within.

Ultimately, the matter would need to be dealt with. Senaya gathered here, as did others, though most were wary of the old trees. Senaya, though — she feared nothing, and had told him, when he asked, that certain herbs gathered from beneath the shadow of the elder trees had more virtue than those found in the tamer part of the forest.

Still, the question remained him — was today the day that Cael alone would enter the dark and silent wood, in pursuit of the trees' child? Or ought he return tomorrow, with a brace of his fellow rangers in support?

The scent was strong, feeding his hesitation. It was as if his quarry tarried in the shadows, watching him.

Taunting him? he wondered. Judging? There was no taint of fear upon the air, and that. . .was troubling.

Cautiously, curiously, he moved along the edge of the trees, just beyond the shadows' cold touch, and he came by that way to a small dug-out place, half-concealed by vegetation, and a small tumble of stone. He paused, for wolves often went to earth in such places to give birth.

Testing the air, he scented rock, and green things, and dust. If the place had once been a den, it was a den no longer.

He approached, and knelt at the opening to look within. The small space was empty, save for brittle bones, long gnawed clean and sifted over with silver sand. He sat back on his heels, then, looking up into the canopy, seeing how close the shadow of the elder trees fell, to this spot; this abandoned wolf's den.

"I found you alone, in the den, with bones about, and no need upon you," he recalled his foster mother's tale of his discovery. "You made no protest when I lifted you up and wrapped you in my sash to bear away."

His throat closed; it was hard to breathe; impossible to scent. Here? She had found him *here*, so near the elder wood that the shadow might well have fallen across the entry-way? And she had never told him?

But wait.

He felt Senaya's cool common sense rise in his blood, banishing panic. He had breath again, and the breeze brought him the information that the one he pursued had retreated further beneath the trees.

His foster mother had not shown him the spot where he had been found, though she had showed him much else among the tame trees. There were, after all, countless wolf-dens and fox-holes in the forest. To think that he had today stumbled upon the one where he — and so close — No.

No.

He was unsettled by the chase, disturbed by the strangeness of the quarry. So, there was one thing decided. He would pursue no further, alone, but return tomorrow, with comrades.

Having taken his decision, he rose, and walked a little further along the shadows' edge, all his senses on alert, seeking anything. . .else that might be amiss.

Satisfied at last that there was no other mischief lurking at the edge of the elder trees, and that the one he had followed here had, indeed, gone away, he turned back, toward the tame wood, and Seafort Village.

#

He had told Senaya about the den, and the wherefore of his fear. She would have felt his distress though their bond, but he wished her to know the process of his thought, especially in light of her mother's assertion that he held some power other than that which they all shared, and used, and — sometimes — plundered.

She heard him out, his Senaya, as they sat together on the bench in their garden, with the evening stealing up, the air cool and damp and tasting of the sea. When he had said all that was in his mind, she put him some few questions, then, setting her arms around him, drew his head down to her breast.

They rested thus while dusk grew into darkness. He was content enough to lie where she had put him; he might, indeed, have fallen quite asleep, save that he felt her thinking, through their bond, and it made him uneasy, that she need think so long, and so hard, upon the matter.

"Cael," she said, at last, and her felt her lips brush his forehead. "You know that you are my heart and that I love you beyond all else."

These were words that ought to have warmed; instead, they chilled him, and he would have sat up, so that he could look into her face, but her arms tightened, and he lay obedient, opening himself as much as possible to her through their bond; his nose bringing him the scent of her determination.

"I know that you love more than I love myself," he murmured. He felt a shiver along their bond; a flash of brilliant heat — and then he did sit up, breaking her grip without effort, and catching her hands in his when she would have embraced him again.

"Cael?"

"Your power rises," he said, looking down into her face. The glow suffused her, illuminating her from within, so that her face became like a moon, indeed, and brightened their little garden.

"Do you fear me?" she asked.

"No," he said, tasting truth on the back of his tongue.

"What do you think that I plan to do?" came the next question, and to that he could only shake his head.

What could his Senaya *not* do, once her will was roused? He could only marvel upon her, and love her the more.

"You are beyond me," he told her, and kissed her glowing cheek, feeling her skin warm against his lips.

"Not that," she said. "Never that, my heart. I raise my power in order to properly ask a boon."

"A boon? We are one, Senaya; there is no need for asking between us!"

"In this thing, there is."

He felt her fingers flex against his palms, as she raised her face to meet his eyes.

"I would ask bride-right, my Cael."

For a moment, he was at a loss, and then he recalled it. Bride-right was more, and less, than the bond they now enjoyed, and it required permission. For what Senaya would do was capture his essence as he stood upon this hour and this day; and hold it within her own essence, as. . .a seed; a possible Cael who might be called into existence with the appropriate application of power. It was a thing not much used among the village-folk, who followed simple ways, but rather more used among the Great Ones, the lords and the ladies and the High Ozali, who had need to protect their power, and their holdings.

Cael drew a breath, and it was on his tongue-tip, the denial.

And then he bethought himself again.

Senaya wished to carry his essence, with its strange power, within herself, cuddled against her very soul.

It was, he realized, understanding her purpose in a flash, it was the most potent way available to her; to prove to him that she believed him no monster, or unnatural thing born from the spite of the elder trees.

And he — how could he doubt himself, when she carried him in her soul? It was a very great gift Senaya proposed to give to him — to them. All of their undertakings would be stronger, because of it.

He smiled at her then, and bent, only a little, to tenderly kiss her mouth. Then, he relinquished her hands and straightened his back.

Looking into her eyes, he smiled again.

"Yes," he said, and felt her power rise over him, and break, like a mighty wave against a stone.

#

It took the three Seafort rangers and three from Stonehold to track and trap the child of the elder trees, which had been fearsome, indeed. Both headwomen and three healers were required to unmake it.

When the thing was done, the folk of both villages came together for feasting, and merry-making, and the sharing about of power.

After the vanquishing of fear, and the celebration of victory, the affairs of both villages, and all the folk of them, slipped back into routine.

Of Senaya the healer and Cael the Ranger, it was said that their bond grew stronger with every sunrise. Certainly, Cael found it so; Senaya's love was the constant star around which his life revolved; he was content; at peace in a way he had not thought possible. The village was all the world he wanted or needed; he felt himself perfectly fixed, and aptly rooted for the whole of his life.

And so he might have remained, had his duty taken him into the woods, rather than across the pastureland. He was to meet a husbandman there, and assist with mending a warding that his animals had grown too wise to heed. It was a fine day, with the taste of the ocean on the breeze. He strode on, lightfoot with joy, when, piercing even the jubilation of the merrybells, came the call of a horn, closely followed by the belling of hounds.

Frowning, he paused, his hand against the trunk of a tree, listening until the horn sounded again.

No bone-made hunting horn, that. The tone was too high, with a hard edge that was only lent by metal. He had heard its like before, but only once. On that occasion, he had yet been serving as his foster mother's apprentice. She had drawn him away from the sound and the hunt, and when he had asked her why, she had looked on him, grim-eyed, and said that it was a horning — the lord's business and none of theirs.

He was his own man now, and had long ago learnt that the great lords in their power and their arrogance did sometimes hold those who displeased them in some manner until there was a house party or other gathering of their allies and peers. Then would the unfortunate prisoner be brought forth and a working performed to give them

the seeming of a hart, or a fox, or some other prey. In that form they would be hunted.

And in that form they would die.

He took a breath, recalling his foster mother's wisdom, for surely such a matter was beyond him, as were all the doings of the great.

Again the horn sounded, and the hounds shouted, much nearer now. He hesitated, listening with sharp ears, trying to gauge the progress of the hunt, and whether he ought turn aside.

Another breath, the breeze against his face, bringing him the tang of the ocean — and another scent, that set his hackles up.

For it was *man* he scented — laboring and afraid. That could only be the prey, and what the great lord Aeronymous was about to set his good hunting hounds upon a *man*, Cael had no notion.

But he intended to stop it.

He was already running, the scent full in his nose; the belling of hounds in his ears. His chosen course would intersect the path of the man and the dogs. If the quarry kept the pace, and Cael did not twist a leg in a goper-hole, then all could be managed: He would buy the prey time, though he doubted much profit would come of it; and he would prevent the dogs from tasting man-flesh.

Ahead of him, a white hart flashed from behind a small stand of trees. Cael threw himself forward, the breeze bringing him the unmistakeable scent of man. He spun, digging the heels of his boots into the ground, facing back the way the hart had run.

Already, he could see the lead dogs, legs extended over the ground as if they were flying. They ran silent, now, which meant they had sighted their quarry. Cael settled himself more firmly onto the ground, and opened his arms.

It occurred to him, very distantly, that he was mad, to set himself between a hunting pack and its prey. These were no easy-going and garrulous village dogs such as he had known all his life. These — these were trained predators. Best outcome, they would flow around him, and shortly bring down the prey.

Worst, he would be mauled — or killed.

Despite the distant realization of his madness, he was not afraid. He was confident and at peace. They would neither harm him nor discount him, those swift-approaching beasts, with their long legs and their razor teeth. They would heed him; and he would keep them safe.

The pack leader was upon him, leaping from a distance, growl drowning the shriek of the merrybells. He caught the beast by the front legs and held him, looking deep into brown eyes, catching and holding the intelligence there.

There came the sense of contact, much as with the village dogs; the leader asserting his superiority — and Cael asserting his own. Slowly, Cael impressed his will; impressed calmness; impressed sense, for this noble fellow — this Scartooth — he was no man-killer, but an honest dog, a strong leader, a mighty hunter. Cael approved of Scartooth, and Scartooth approved of Cael. Scartooth was happy to be with Cael.

Scartooth, indeed, would do all and anything that Cael asked, for Cael was leader, and Scartooth so acknowledged him.

. . .by the time the horses and the lords arrived, the pack was lolling on the meadow-grass at his feet, and Cael was softly caressing Scartooth's ragged ears.

#

The great ones burned so brightly that Cael wished to close his eyes; the weight of their power like to crush him to his knees.

However, he neither averted his eyes, nor knelt before their radiance. It was his to protect the pack; and so he stood tall and met the sea-blue eyes of the forward rider.

"Well, here's a twist," said the other great one, who sat a stone-grey horse like a boulder come to life. "What's to do, Aeronymous?"

"Why, now we test our skill at tracking," blue-eyed Aeronymous said, his voice light and even, as if finding his hunters taking their ease in the middle of a hunt was entirely unsurprising, even expected.

"You, boy! Take the pack to their kennel, and tend them till I call!"

Power struck him, hard, augmenting the light command; he felt the need to obey, precisely, sink into his bones, and become his own will.

He bowed to the honor of Lord Aeronymous. Straightening, he patted Scartooth on the shoulder.

"Home," he murmured.

The dog moved forward, Cael at his side, and the others leapt to their feet to follow.

The horses and the lords swept around them, on the trail of the one who wore the seeming of a white hart. Last to pass him was one who smelled of the pack. Scartooth favored him with a glance, before nipping a youngling who lay still in the meadow grass.

"What have you done?" whispered the man — the dog-master, he must be, Cael realized.

"Prevented the dogs from learning that man is prey," he answered, more sharply than he had intended.

The dog-master's face paled. He licked his lips, then kicked his horse and rode away through the silver dust raised by the lords' horses.

Cael shrugged, and said again to Scartooth, "Home."

#

There had been no compulsion that they hurry, only that they return. Thus they went leisurely, hunting on the move. The dogs knew their business, and by the time they passed through the small gate, there were three rabbits and a brace of forest-hens in Cael's game sack.

They crossed the green, Cael at the head of the pack, and Scar-tooth at his side, his ragged ears held high, and his head at the level of Cael's belt. The compulsion was stronger now, to find the kennel quickly, but not so strong that he was unable to stop when an arms-man approached, and said, quietly, "Stay."

There was a little power in that command, but nothing to over-ride the lord's geas.

Cael stopped of his own will and looked into the man's eyes.

"Who are you?" the arms-man asked.

"Cael of Seafort," he answered. "Lord Aeronymous sends me to kennel the hounds, and to bide with them till he calls."

The arms-man nodded slowly, and made as if to step back.

"Hold," Cael said, and offered the game sack. "For the kitchen, if you would. I do not think I can deviate so much." Indeed, it would seem that he had already remained in one spot too long; his feet were shifting against the grass.

"I'll take it," the arms-man said. "Go — the lord is not gentle with those who try him."

"My thanks," Cael said, and the pack moved on, through the gate in good order, and the young ones running for the water, while Cael kept walking to the very center of the place, whereupon the will of Aeronymous released him, and he heard the gate snap shut at his back.

#

He lay against Scartooth's back, the rest of the pack lying as close as possible, their joy in his presence warming him as much as the heat from their bodies. The dogs, simple and honest as they were, slept.

He, less simple and perhaps not so honest as he had always supposed himself, lay awake, staring up at the stars like jewels in the night sky.

The bond he shared with Senaya seemed. . .less strong in this place that was laced with so much power, and so many workings that his skin itched, and his eyes burned. He did his best to tend it, the bond; Senaya might not know where he was, nor how long he might be away, but he was determined that she not be in fear for his life. Lord Aeronymous — well, there had been a warning, had there not, from the arms-man? Lord Aeronymous was not gentle with those who thwarted him. He must, therefore, expect to be punished. He did not think that the lord would unmake him; it seemed to him that his impertinence in interrupting the lord's pleasure was not worth that. There had, however, been the other lord, before whom Aeronymous had been disadvantaged. . .

No, it was impossible to guess what Lord Aeronymous might do, he decided, and his thoughts turned again to his determination to stop the hunt, and to preserve the integrity of the dogs.

Since childhood, he had easy discourse with the village dogs; they deferred to him, and mentioned odd smells and movements to him. That was merely. . .who he was. He did understand that others did not enjoy the same level of intimacy with the dogs — even Senaya did not. But, then, Senaya's gift was healing; she had no need to speak with dogs.

That he had dared placed himself between a pack and its prey — that amazed him yet, and, at the same time, it surprised him not at all, that the dogs had come to him, and placed their wills in service to his. He had expended no power; he had merely. . .stretched himself beyond the familiar mold of husband and ranger, as if he had straightened to his full height after years of standing stooped.

He heard footsteps, coming toward the kennel, and a subtle chime, as if metal struck metal. Around him, the dogs lifted their heads, noses up, testing the air. He did the same, scenting power, and beneath it, the scent of the arms-man who had relieved him of the game-bag.

Cael stood, and Scartooth stood, also. He placed his hand on the hound's shoulder, and murmured to the rest of them, "Stay. Friends."

"Cael of Seafort," came the voice of Aeronymous. "Come forth alone to make an account of your actions to your liege lord."

He felt the power snatch at him, jerking him forward like a doll. Apparently, Lord Aeronymous did not care to give a man the choice of obeying from his own heart.

Pulled by power, he came to the kennel's door, and only then realized that Scartooth paced him yet.

"Stay," he murmured.

The hound whined, close in his throat, echoing the distress growing in Cael's breast. Whined once — and obeyed.

On the green, Lord Aeronymous stood at the center of a nimbus of light, his green curls all tumbled 'round his shoulders, as if he were come fresh from his bed.

"Stand," he said, his voice as cold as ocean spray, and Cael stopped where he was. He heard the arms-man move, and the sound of the kennel's gate being firmly shut.

"So, Cael of Seafort, why have you not come to my attention ere this?" asked Aeronymous.

"My lord, there was no need, that you notice one ranger more than another."

"But such an *unusual* ranger," Aeronymous murmured, and then snapped, "What did you do to my hounds, sirrah?"

That was accompanied by a lash of power, burning as it broke across his cheek.

Cael took a breath.

"I prevented them from learning that man is prey. They are good dogs — hunting dogs. To use them to hunt men — it was a corruption of their service, my lord."

He braced himself for another blow, and was mildly surprised when it did not come.

"The criminal they chased was horned, exactly to prevent this lesson of man as prey from being learnt."

Cael shook his head.

"He smelled like a man yet, my lord. I caught the scent myself. The dogs knew what they hunted."

There was a long pause, in which power snapped and glittered, but none struck him.

Inside his halo of light, Aeronymous inclined his stately head.

"For the sake of my hounds, I thank you, Cael Dog-Friend. Come with me now."

With that, Aeronymous turned and marched off, a line of power sunk deep into Cael's chest, so that he was pulled along in the lord's wake, like a child's toy. The arms-man kept pace, and Cael smelled his dismay.

He scented them in the instant before the lord exerted his power, compelling Cael to leap down into a pit. Smelled them; heard them — and, landing with bent knees, saw them, as the lord threw his nimbus wide.

Wolves.

Coats brindled, and eyes red-shot, half-mad with their confinement. They growled, all three as one. Cael dropped to one knee, seeking the red gaze of the wolf before him. Teeth showed, the growl came to a crescendo; and Cael felt the connection made; breathed in, waiting. . .

The wolf threw himself onto his back, paws waving in the air. Cael leaned in to rub the lean belly, while the other two jostled him, licking his face and hands.

Kneeling, he opened his heart, and allowed their untamed nature to rise into him, stirring his blood, freshening his courage.

"Cael of Seafort, come to me!"

He felt the tug of the lord's will, augmenting the command. He resisted the compulsion, though doing so waked a pain like a dagger through his breast.

"My lord!" He called out. "I obey you, but in my time. There is delicate business afoot, and I cannot say what will happen, if I am suddenly removed from it."

There was a slight pause, in which he thought he heard the arms-man gasp. Then came the voice of Aeronymous once more.

"Do not by any means endanger yourself," he said. "You become precious to me, Cael the Wolf, and I would not see thee harmed. I leave here at your service Erdin, my arms-man sworn. He will lower a rope to you when you ask for it. You will — in your time, of course! — place yourself in his hands, for he has my orders concerning you."

"Yes," Cael whispered, drinking in what the wolves would give him: stealth, cunning, loyalty, fierce devotion.

Wolf ears heard the lord's departure; wolf senses noted the man left behind, shivering in the cold sea air. Cael and the wolves dreamed red dreams and gold together, until they faded.

The wolves slept. Cael rose, stiff with long kneeling, walked to the edge of the pit and called quietly for Erdin to lower the rope.

#

Dawn was painting bronze streaks across the velvet sky when he was ushered — fed, bathed, and dressed in tunic and leggings provided by the House — into the presence of his lord. Into, as Erdin whispered to him before he knocked upon the door, my lord's private chambers. Erdin misliked this private meeting, though Cael was at a loss to know why. He might have asked the arms-man, but the door swung open then, and they entered a room done 'round in shelves, each groaning beneath a weight of books. Aeronymous sat in a white conch by the window, a book open, but unregarded upon his lap. His head was turned, the green curls orderly now; and it appeared that he watched the progress of the dawn.

"My lord," said Erdin, "the ranger Cael is here."

"In his own time," my lord murmured, without turning his head. "Leave him; and find yourself some rest."

Erdin hesitated, and it seemed to Cael that he would speak, save Aeronymous, his face turned toward the window, tipped his head just slightly, as if listening closely for some particular sound.

The arms-man swallowed and bowed.

"Yes, my lord," he said, and shot a sharp glance at Cael before he strode away into the hallway.

The door closed behind him.

Slowly, then, the shell-chair turned, until Aeronymous was fully facing the room. Cael met the sea-blue eyes, then, recalling himself, bowed to the lord's honor.

When he straightened, he met the lord's eyes again, and waited.

"You are bold," Aeronymous said musingly. "Perhaps Erdin failed of telling you that I find boldness. . .impertinent."

"He did say so, sir," Cael admitted, not wishing to cause the arms-man harm.

"But you chose to ignore him. Or you do not think it imperti-
nent that a ranger boldly meet the eyes of a lord."

There seemed nothing to say to this that might not be construed
as continuing impertinence — Erdin had warned him, also, that
Aeronymous counted slights with a heavy hand.

"Well," Aeronymous said, closing his book. It rose from his knee,
and wafted to the shelf on the right of the chair, where it inserted itself into the space from which it must have been summoned.

Cael kept his eyes turned toward the lord, his gaze somewhat
averted, so that he did not give challenge by a direct stare.

"Well," Aeronymous said again. "You have convinced me, Cael
the Wolf, that you must become attached to my household."

Cael drew a breath. "I had no wish to do so, my lord," he said,
softly, his gaze averted.

"Of that, I am certain," Aeronymous said. "Indeed, I had thought
to let you go with a beating, and a tithe of your power given in liege-
gift. But there is no help for either of us; you must become mine."

Panic rose in him; he quelled it, and bowed, as courtly as he was
able.

"My lord, I have a place, and there I serve you well. I –"

Aeronymous waved a hand.

"Yes, yes," he said impatiently. "You have a bond-mate, and a life,
and your duty, wherein you served me, *in your way*, I make no doubt."
The blue eyes had taken on grey, as if storm clouds moved over the
ocean. "You ought to have thought of these things before you turned
my dogs from their task, and brought yourself to my attention. You
ought, perhaps, to have allowed the wolves to kill you. But you did
not the one, and failed of the other, and thus the case falls to me."

He stood, then, power outlining his form, and his curls stirring,
as if in a sea-breeze.

"You are too dangerous a man, Cael the Wolf, to be left to your own will and judgment. You would ever be a blade at my back. If blade you would be, then you will be safely sheathed, and hung upon *my* belt."

"My lord, I mean you no harm. I –"

"Silence!"

A blow struck his chin, snapping his mouth shut. Within that sealed cavern, his tongue began to burn.

He reached, blindly, to his own poor store of power, bringing it, icy, into his mouth. Surprisingly, the lord allowed it; he allowed the fire to be quenched. But he did not allow Cael to unseal his lips.

"Hear me, now, for there is a choice before you, one of the few that remain to you. Either you will release your bond of your own will, or I will break it, of mine. Understand that some damage might be done, if I am the author of this action, and I think you will agree that it would be a sad pity, were Seafort deprived of its healer.

Choose carefully, Cael the Wolf."

His blood was hot with his risen power; he was terrified for Senaya — and as before, there was neither thought nor uncertainty, as he straightened into that other power, which was his alone — and called.

From the kennels, came the belling of hounds.

From further yet, came the howling of wolves.

He felt himself expand further still, and in some interior room a lap-dog began to yip. He would free himself; he would be not be bound here; he —

A blade of power slashed through him, and he screamed, his lips tearing open, before he fell, insensible, to the foam-colored rug.

#

"Wake!"

He tasted blood as he straightened his back — and felt the bite of restraints, around arms and legs; his throat was gripped, tight and cold, and when he moved his head to worry at it, he heard the clank of chain.

At last he opened his eyes, saw one end of the chain in the hand of Aeronymous, and felt the metal biting into his skin.

"Are you a fool, Cael the Wolf? Speak!"

"No, my lord," he heard himself say, though he had willed no answer.

"I take leave to doubt it. Did you think to best me? Did you think to break away? Rousing my own dogs against me, in the depths of my own holding? Would you slay your lord? Put your paltry, peasant happiness before the command of your liege? However you came to be, your only purpose is to *obey me*. You live at my whim, and when you have served me to the fullness of your meager ability, I will drink you down in one quaff, Cael the Wolf. Do these things please you? Speak!"

"Yes, master," he heard himself say, and hated the words.

"You have now demonstrated to both of us why it is that you must on no account be allowed your own will. Perhaps it was necessary. Allow me now to recall to you your penultimate choice. Do you break the bond, or do I break the healer? You have shown me no reason to be gentle."

Senaya. No, he would not give Senaya to the lord's cruelty. But. . .to break faith with her whom he shared. . .everything? Such a sundering must unmake one — or both! — as close as their sharing had been.

He took a breath, and looked to his lord.

"Speak," said Aeronymous.

"I will do it," he said, his voice hoarse.

"Then be about it, quickly!"

He closed his eyes, and found the bond lying hard against his heart, quivering with Senaya's distress. Her mother was with her, and the eldest of her sisters. Good. They would do what was needful, and keep her away from harm.

The proper way to break a bond, is to cut it in the middle, so that neither side suffers more from the severing than is. . .needful.

Cael brought his will and his intent to his own heart, concentrating on the bond until it filled his entire awareness.

He brought the knife of his will down, severing the bond with a single strike.

And screamed again, as power poured out of him like blood, and his heart shattered in his breast. Blackness overtook him; he embraced it. Somewhere, he heard a dog howling, and in the woods, deep in the woods, shrouded in emerald light, he saw something move four-footed among the fallen leaves, and rise up on two legs to face the wolf. . .

. . .wolf. . .

It was cold. The wolf faded, and the wood. He reached out to touch Senaya — and found. . .nothing.

#

Fire fell out of cold nothingness, assaulting his last fluttering thought. Power poured into him, scalding; scouring. His mouth was filled with salt, and his ears with the crashing of waves. His sundered heart was fire-forged; melted and made whole; the howl that he heard was his own, until — at last and again — he heard nothing at all.

#

He came to himself. His cheek was pressed to the rug; the bonds and the collar were gone. There was a. . .weight at the center of his chest, but there was no pain.

There was no pain.

"You may rise and look upon your liege lord, Cael the Wolf."

The voice thrilled him; he rose eager, and raised his eyes, gasping in an agony of love. He dropped to his knees, tears springing to his eyes, but he was not ashamed, for was this not his liege-lord, whom he loved above all else?

"Are you in truth my faithful wolf?"

"*Yes*, my lord."

"It pleases me to hear it. Raise your face to me — yes. Do you love me, Cael?"

"Only you, my lord."

Aeronymous stepped forward and held out his slim hand.

"Swear to me, if that is your will."

Of course it was his will! He placed his hand into the hand of his lord, and gazed up into those sea-blue eyes.

"I, Cael, do swear upon my soul that I will keep faith with Aeronymous and never cause him harm. I will defend him and reverence him and in all things obey him; and stand his man forevermore."

There was a faint boom, as if a door had shut, and a sharp pain at the center of his chest — gone before he could gasp. He felt a glow of happiness.

"Excellent," his lord said. "We shall never part, Cael the Wolf. Your oath binds you to Aeronymous, for lack of whom you will die. Does that please you?"

Something stirred at the back of his mind, showing teeth in a silent snarl, but that was as nothing before the joy that suffused him.

"I am pleased, my liege."

A smile came onto those cold lips.

"Hear me, then. You will serve me as Master of Hounds. The first task you are given is to become court-wise and handy, for my Master of Hounds will sit at the second highest table, and be the equal of those who style themselves noble. You will be my eyes and my ears, and you will report all that you have heard, to me, and me alone."

Behind him, he heard the door open, but he remained on his knees, looking up into his lord's face. He could have remained so for the rest of his life, and wanted for nothing else.

However, his lord had other necessities.

"Rise," Aeronymous said, and he did so, anticipating the opportunity to serve.

Aeronymous gestured, and one came forward, splendid in courtly dress, scented with book dust; his power heavy with knowledge.

"You will go with this one," his lord said, "and learn all that is taught to you."

"Yes, my lord." He bowed; straightened, and hesitated.

"Speak," said Aeronymous.

"Yes, my lord. I only wonder. . .Will I *see* you?"

Once again Aeronymous was seen to smile.

"I will be with you always, my wolf, for are we not of one heart?"

#

He was an exemplary wolf — intelligent, loyal, and fierce. In those early days, he mastered every lesson set to him, quickly and thoroughly. History, custom, court courtesy and dialect, the deportment expected of one who sat among lords — those things he leaned easily. Arms work and hand-to-hand — those he barely needed to learn; it was if he had been born with an innate understanding of such matters. Horsemanship, however, had been a long road, for horses did not like him. Even now he rode but rarely, though he had long since mastered the spell-work to force his mount to calm obedience.

Having been schooled in the basics, he was placed as his lord had said — at the second table, among those who were great, but who had ambition. His listened, as he had been directed, and he repeated what his keen ears heard, to no one but Aeronymous. Indeed, his happiest moments were those spent sitting at his lord's feet in the private parlor, reporting and then listening as Aeronymous told over what this or that nugget might mean; who must be culled, and who left to continue until it was seen what others joined with him, in an attempt to bring Aeronymous down from his high seat, drink his power, and set themselves up as Sea Ozali in his stead.

He had brought the tales of such plots to his lord, as he was bound to do; and he stood by his lord's side, when punishment was extracted. That, too, was something to learn, but Aeronymous did not always — or even often — mete death to those who would have gladly served him that dish.

Of one, he drew power, rendering his enemy invalid and scarce able to defend himself. It would have been kinder merely to kill him; but his lord Aeronymous was not kind.

It was *more effective* to return him, trembling and frail, to the ranks of his sometime allies. To them he spoke, for the few days longer that he managed to survive; he told them of the cold will of Aeronymous, and his power that was too great to be taken. So, he taught them, if neither fear nor respect, at least caution.

Of another plotter, he merely drew the names of her compatri-
ots, and let her return to her place, unscathed; undiminished in hon-
or. Not so, those whose names had been taken; those, Aeronymous
broke slowly, partaking of their power a sip at a time, savoring their
suffering. He had required Cael by his side for this, and fed him also
tit-bits of power; scraps from the feast table.

Still a third, he reached out to at a state dinner, and drew his
power all at once, killing him where he sat; the thing so deftly done
that none but Cael understood it had happened until the guests rose
from table, for dancing.

In this way, by these stratagems, did Aeronymous keep his seat
and grow his power. He was an awful lord, but one who protected all
within his care.

Save they did not try him.

For his part, Cael was content. The love he held for his lord was
constant; it could not be otherwise. He knew that those other ser-
vants of Aeronymous feared him, but it mattered little. There were
those who did not fear him, and who welcomed him with uncompli-
cated joy. He visited the dogs often, as this thing had not been denied
him by his lord, and he reveled in their simple honesty.

He was, indeed, on his way to the kennels even now.

It was rare for him to be free at so early an hour in the evening,
but Lord Aeronymous had lately acquired a new favorite, and it was
his pleasure to retire them early for disport and enjoyment. This was
the third favorite Cael had seen; and he wished she would eventually
be cast from the lord's bedchamber as the first had been — pleased,
somewhat increased in power, and hung about with trinkets.

The second. . .had not fared so well. He had presumed upon the
lord's infatuation, mistaking indulgence for weakness.

Aeronymous was never weak. And it had been, Cael had reflected at the time, a terrible thing to have fallen from favorite to traitor, for the lord had been as full with his fury as he had been with his brighter passion.

Cael shivered as he made his way toward the kennel, and not only because the ocean air was chill. It was well, he thought, that Aeronymous had fixed his own regard and nature in the moment of his resurrection. Whatever he had lost in his love for the lord, at least he risked no death such as had been meted the second favorite.

He came 'round the corner of the house, following the path that skirted the kitchen garden — and froze, a step echoing in his ear.

There was no footstep among the House which was strange to him, but this — a soft footfall by nature, purposeful by intent; familiar, and beloved, long before he had come to the House of Aeronymous.

The breeze danced 'round the edge of the house, bringing him her scent, and he spun, horror replacing his content, searching the path with his keen, hound's eyes. . .

She stepped out from the kitchen doorway, and stood in the center of the path, her hands folded beneath her cloak, and her dark hair lying loose upon her shoulders.

"Senaya!" He could not move — but she did, walking slowly down the path to him, outlined by the meager glow of her power.

"So, you remember me. It was said in the village that Lord Aeronymous had rent your past from you."

He shook his head, trembling now, horror rooting him yet to the path.

"I remember," he said. "Senaya –"

"You glow like the moon, my Cael. Surely, you are a lord, yourself."

"No," he said harshly. "I am my lord's lapdog, with his collar 'round my heart."

It frightened him, that he spoke those words. He had known, of course; Aeronymous had not taken his memories, nor hidden the manner of his binding — that would have been kind. Still, he had been content to let the knowledge lie sleeping beneath what he had become.

"I see it," Senaya said, stopping now that they were toe to toe. "He has hurt you, my Cael, and grievously. You were not meant, ever, to be chained."

"It is too late, as you must see. Senaya — you must not bide here! He will — I do not know what he will do, but he threatened once to break you, and –"

"And you would not allow it. I know; I was there with you, through the bond, until the moment you broke us asunder. I thought then that I would die. My mother thought that, surely, you had." She paused, tipping her head, perhaps to study him more closely.

"My sister said that you *wished* to die."

"I had. I. . .did. My lord caught my soul before it took flight."

"And bound it to his service, twisting you as he did so."

"Senaya, this is of no use. I am lost to you, as if I had died, in truth. Go, I beg you –"

"You are afraid," she murmured. "For me. This is more than I had hoped for."

"Should I not be afraid for you? I love you!"

He gasped, pain searing him, as if someone had wrung his living heart in a vise.

"Cael?"

He shook his head, breathing against the agony until it grew bearable, hearing his blurted words again, tasting the simple truth of them. And that was worse — far worses than mere pain. If anyone had heard, who would bear the tale to Aeronymous; if the sea-breeze wafted those words to his lord's sharp ears. . .

"Senaya, you *must* go."

She smiled and lay her hand on his shoulder.

"Why, and so I shall, very soon. I had only wished to see you again, my Cael; and to give you a gift."

A gift? He had no need of gifts; his one pressing need was to see her safe away. Already, he was planning; he might send Scartooth and Vinja with her, to guard her way back to the village. They were good dogs, and true; they would let nothing harm her.

"Peace, my love," she murmured. "Recall, when we were bonded, I asked bride-right, and you granted it?"

"Yes. . ." He remember the feel of her power enveloping him; how he had trembled at her strength. . .

"We are no longer bonded, and I wish to marry again. Thus, I return to you your nature."

"My nature." He dared to extend a hand, and touch her dear face. "Senaya, hear me. I am a child of the old wood; an unnatural thing. What you hold is. . .a monster. Cast it from you."

She turned her cheek into his caress. "No monster, but an honest man, and true, who even now plots to see me safely away, discounting any cost to himself." She took a breath, and moved one careful step back from him.

"Hear me, now, Cael who was bondmate to Senaya; this thing that our lord has imposed upon you — it is not love, no matter how great a burden it casts upon your heart. Allow it to rule you and you will become a monster, indeed. I return to you your nature, that you may have a true guide, untainted by our lord's power."

Her power flared, and broke, a minor wavelet, spending at his feet. There was no other sensation, save his sadness, that he should have so far outgrown her; who had only wished to be her equal.

It struck him then, like a rock to the chest; power flared, igniting him, blood and bone. Senaya swam in his vision, and he heard a dog whine, near at hand.

His sight left him entirely as he went to his knees on the path; he felt Senaya's arms come 'round him tightly, and her lips seek his.

"No. . ." he managed, feeling his power hungrily yearn toward her. "Senaya. . ."

"Yes," she whispered. "I would marry again, my Cael; I would never again be without you."

His younger self, burning yet into his bones, ached for her, his power, gained from Aeronymous, hungered to consume her. He trembled, and sought to put her from him, but all she need do was press her lips to his ear and murmur two fateful words.

"Freely given."

She flowed into him, cool and wise and constant — so little, and so quickly absorbed by the hungry fires of his power.

He felt her diminish in his grasp, and held her closer, but she melted even as his arms tightened. Crying out, he wrenched his eyes open, and beheld her, translucent in the moonlight, the stars glowing through her, like jewels.

Then came a breeze, tasting of salt and seaweed. . .

And she was gone.

Cael, called the Wolf, knelt on the path in the moonlight, his heart like a stone in his breast; and next to it, another stone, as light as the first was heavy.

And flowing through the currents of his power, cool and wise and strong, he felt her, and knew they would never again be parted.

Sharon Lee

–end–

Author's Notes
The Wolf's Bride

So, this is what we in the business call a "discovery story." It was written in August 2013, right after I turned in the final draft of *Carousel Seas*.

For those who have not read the Archers Beach Carousel trilogy by Sharon Lee, Cael the Wolf makes his appearance about mid-way through *Carousel Seas*. He's a very strong character, and I liked him a great deal. So much, in fact, that I thought, for a mad, halcyon few months, that I would write a book about him.

To do that, I needed to know where Cael came from. I knew he was a native of the Land of the Flowers, and had served Kate's grandfather, the Sea Ozali Aeronymous, for a long time, and not entirely of his own free will.

So, I set out to get a feel for how things operated in the Land of Flowers, which is touched on only very lightly in the novels; and to find out how Cael came to serve Aeronymous, who is. . .*not* a Nice Guy. . .and yet remain basically honorable and kind.

The result of all that is "The Wolf's Bride."

And, yes; it turns out that the Land of the Flowers is even stranger than Kate had let on, in our discussions together.

I'd still like, one day, to write a book about Cael, after he arrives in Archers Beach and takes up his duties there.

In the meantime, I hope you enjoyed the story.

—Sharon Lee
January 2016

About the Author

Sharon Lee is the author of a contemporary, Maine-based fantasy trilogy set in the only slightly fictional town of Archers Beach: *Carousel Tides, Carousel Sun*, and *Carousel Seas*, published by Baen Books and available in trade paper, electronic and audiobook editions. She has also written two Maine-based mystery novels—*Barnburner* and *Gunshy*—and numerous shorter stories.

Both of the short stories in this echapbook are set in Archers Beach. Two previous echapbooks—*Surfside* and *The Gift of Magic*—contain four more Archers Beach short stories.

In addition to her solo work, Sharon has co-authored 24 novels of science fiction and fantasy with her husband, Steve Miller. Twenty of those works are set in their bestselling Liaden Universe® series.

Sharon lives in Maine with her husband, four cats, and rather a number of books. You can keep up with her through The Blog Without a Name at sharonleewriter.com.

Other Works by Sharon Lee

Crystal Soldier
Crystal Dragon
Fledgling
Saltation
Mouse and Dragon
Ghost Ship
Dragon Ship
Necessity's Child
Trade Secret
Dragon in Exile
Alliance of Equals
The Gathering Edge (coming in 2017)
LIADEN UNIVERSE® SHORT STORY COLLECTIONS
A Liaden Universe Constellation: Volume 1
A Liaden Universe Constellation: Volume 2
A Liaden Universe Constellation: Volume 3
THE FEY DUOLOGY
Duainfey
Longeye
OTHER UNIVERSES
The Tomorrow Log
Sword of Orion

The above novels, published by Baen Books, are available wherever books are sold, in paper, electronic, and audio editions

The short story collections are available in paper and ebook editions

For more Lee and Miller titles please visit Pinbeam Books: visit www.pinbeambooks.com

Thank you

for your interest in
and support of
our work
Sharon Lee and Steve Miller

Don't miss out!

Click the button below and you can sign up to receive emails whenever Sharon Lee publishes a new book. There's no charge and no obligation.

https://books2read.com/r/B-A-MRWB-ZVNK

Connecting independent readers to independent writers.